The Lost City's Treasure

The Time-Traveling Kids, Volume 3

Jason Bland

Published by Jason Bland, 2024.

THE LOST CITY'S TREASURE

First edition. November 15, 2024.

Written by Jason Bland.

CHAPTER 1

THE MAP IN THE MIST

The dense jungle buzzed with life as Emma, Rami, Zoe, and Liam trudged through the thick undergrowth, their boots sinking into the damp earth. Towering trees stretched endlessly upward, their canopies weaving a shield against the blazing sun. Shafts of light broke through the greenery, illuminating their path in golden streaks.

"Remind me again why we couldn't just find a lost city somewhere less... sticky?" Zoe muttered, swiping at a mosquito buzzing near her ear.

Rami chuckled, adjusting the strap of his backpack. "Because ancient civilizations didn't think about bug spray."

Emma, leading the group with the ancient compass in her hand, glanced back. "The compass brought us here for a reason. If the lost city and the eighth stone are real, we're exactly where we need to be."

The compass, an intricate device they had discovered at the Temple of Sands, hummed faintly in her palm. Its needle didn't point north but rather twisted erratically, as if attuned to an unseen force. Every now and then, it would lock in place for a moment, guiding them deeper into the uncharted jungle.

"This doesn't look like the kind of place anyone would build a city," Liam said, brushing aside a low-hanging vine. "It's all trees and vines... and more vines."

Emma slowed, her gaze sweeping the area. "Exactly. If it's a lost city, it's supposed to be hidden."

The group continued their march until they reached a clearing dominated by an ancient stone arch, partially swallowed by creeping moss and vines. Strange carvings adorned its weathered surface—symbols that seemed to shimmer faintly in the dappled light.

"What do you think this is?" Zoe asked, running her fingers over the carvings.

Emma pulled out the notebook she'd been using to sketch their discoveries. "These symbols match some of the ones we saw at the Temple of Sands. It's a language, but... not one I recognize."

"Maybe it's a marker," Rami suggested. "Like a signpost leading to the city."

Before Emma could respond, the compass vibrated in her hand, its needle spinning wildly before pointing directly through the arch. She felt a faint pulse of energy, like an unspoken invitation.

"This is it," Emma whispered, stepping closer. "We're on the right track."

As they passed under the arch, the jungle seemed to shift. The air grew heavier, the sounds of animals and insects fading into an eerie silence. A thick mist rolled in, curling around their legs and making it harder to see more than a few steps ahead.

"I don't like this," Zoe muttered, her voice low. "It's too quiet."

"Stay close," Emma said firmly. "Whatever's ahead, we're facing it together."

They pressed on, the mist growing denser with every step. Shadows danced in the periphery of their vision, shapes that seemed to flicker and vanish when they turned to look. The compass vibrated again, its hum growing louder.

Finally, the mist parted, revealing the outline of a massive structure ahead. The group froze, staring in awe at what lay before them: a towering ziggurat of black stone, its surface covered in glowing blue symbols that pulsed like a heartbeat.

"The lost city," Liam whispered, his voice tinged with awe. "It's real."

But before they could move closer, a loud *crack* split the air, and the ground beneath their feet trembled. Out of the shadows emerged figures cloaked in darkness, their faces hidden by masks shaped like animal skulls. They carried staffs topped with glowing crystals, their movements synchronized and deliberate.

"Who are they?" Zoe hissed, instinctively stepping back.

Rami's voice was barely audible. "Guardians."

One of the figures stepped forward, its staff glowing brighter as it slammed the base against the ground. The symbols on the ziggurat flared to life, casting the clearing in an ethereal glow. The figure spoke in a deep, resonant voice, the words unfamiliar but filled with authority.

Emma felt the weight of the moment settle over her. These guardians were here to protect the city—and whatever secrets it held. The eighth stone was within their grasp, but it was clear that their journey had just become much more perilous.

With a deep breath, Emma tightened her grip on the compass and stepped forward. "We're not here to harm your city," she said, her voice steady. "We're here to uncover the truth and protect its legacy."

The guardians remained silent, their masked faces unreadable. But the leader raised a hand, gesturing for them to follow.

"Guess we're doing this," Liam murmured as they fell into step behind the silent figures. "Into the heart of the lost city."

As they crossed the threshold into the ancient ziggurat, the weight of history—and the challenges ahead—pressed down on them. The jungle had tested their endurance, but the city would test their courage, intelligence, and resolve in ways they couldn't yet imagine.

The adventure had only just begun.

CHAPTER 2

THE CITY OF SHADOWS

The air inside the ziggurat was thick with ancient magic, the temperature dropping dramatically as they moved deeper into the stone labyrinth. The guardians, still wordless and foreboding, led them through narrow hallways lined with murals and carvings, their staffs glowing faintly, lighting the way. The walls were covered with intricate designs—warriors battling mythical creatures, celestial bodies aligned in patterns Emma had never seen before, and what looked like a map of the stars.

"Look at this," Emma whispered, reaching out to trace the intricate designs. The shapes almost seemed to shimmer under her touch. "It's like they were marking the passage of time, but... not in any way I understand."

Rami squinted at the map-like carvings. "This looks like a map of the night sky. Could it be... showing the constellations of this place?"

The misty air seemed to respond to their voices, the shadows flickering and shifting, as though the walls themselves were alive. Zoe glanced nervously over her shoulder, her hand resting on the hilt of her knife. "I don't know about you guys, but this place gives me the creeps."

Liam nodded, his voice soft. "It's like we're being watched."

Before anyone could respond, the lead guardian stopped in front of a massive stone door, its surface adorned with more glowing symbols. With a grunt, the figure lifted a staff and tapped it against the door three times. The symbols on the stone began to shimmer, and with a grinding sound, the door slowly began to open, revealing a vast, cavernous room beyond.

As they stepped into the chamber, the door slammed shut behind them, trapping them in total darkness for a brief moment before the walls flickered to life with a soft, golden light. Emma gasped as the room unfolded before them—an enormous hall with towering pillars, each one carved from a single block of black stone. The ceiling stretched impossibly high, disappearing into shadow. But what captured their attention were the rows of gleaming artifacts and strange objects laid out in glass cases, like treasures from another world.

In the center of the room stood a massive stone pedestal, its surface covered in ancient dust. But atop the pedestal...

"The eighth stone," Emma whispered, almost breathless.

It was unlike any of the stones they had collected so far. It shimmered with an eerie light, its surface covered in intricate, moving patterns that seemed to shift like waves crashing against a distant shore. The moment Emma laid eyes on it, she felt a pull—a magnetic force that seemed to draw her toward it. She stepped forward, but before she could reach out, one of the guardians raised a hand, halting her.

"You must pass the trial," the leader intoned in a low, melodic voice. "Only the worthy may claim the stone. Others will be... lost to time."

The room grew colder, the air thickening with tension. The guardians stepped aside, leaving Emma and her friends to face the unknown.

Rami swallowed, his usual bravado dimming in the face of the trial. "What kind of trial are we talking about?"

The leader of the guardians gestured to the pedestal. "This city was built to guard the treasures of the ancients. The stone is but one part of the puzzle. To take it, you must first understand its power."

A low hum filled the air as the walls began to shift. The golden light flickered, revealing hidden doors along the edges of the room. Each door had a symbol above it—symbols that mirrored the ones they had seen in the temple and the jungle.

Emma stepped forward, drawn to one of the doors. It depicted a spiral, the same shape that had appeared in her visions whenever she held the compass. She turned to her friends. "I think the trial involves these doors. We need to choose the right one."

The others nodded, stepping up beside her. The walls seemed to grow more alive as they approached the doors, the symbols glowing more brightly, as if testing them, daring them to make a mistake.

Zoe was the first to speak. "Do we just pick a door?"

Emma hesitated. "It doesn't seem like that easy. I think we need to figure out what each symbol represents. Maybe each door leads us to a different challenge."

Liam ran his hand over the symbols. "Look, this one looks like the sun rising over the mountains. It could be a test of strength, or survival."

"Or something to do with light," Rami added, glancing over at the second door, which had an image of a vast river flowing toward an ocean. "This one looks like it might be about navigating or understanding the flow of things."

Emma's fingers tingled as she traced the spiral door again. "This one... I think it's about the journey. The unknown paths."

A sudden crack echoed in the room, and all the symbols began to glow in sync, brighter and brighter until the whole chamber shimmered with energy. The guardians took a step back, their faces hidden beneath their masks.

"This is it," Emma said, her voice firm. "We need to choose wisely."

The group stood in silence for a moment, each of them looking at the doors. Rami clenched his fist. "I say we pick the one with the river. It seems like the safest bet. We know how to move with the flow, right?"

Zoe raised an eyebrow. "And you think the river is the easy way?"

Emma, however, felt a pull toward the spiral. There was something about it that spoke to her, something deeper than mere intuition.

"The spiral," she said, her voice steady. "It feels right. We've been through so much already, and each step has led us here. We've faced the unknown before... and now it's time to keep going."

With a deep breath, she approached the door with the spiral symbol. As her fingers brushed against the stone, the air seemed to vibrate with energy. The door slowly creaked open, revealing a dark corridor beyond.

"This is it," Emma said, her voice a mix of determination and uncertainty. "We're taking the next step."

As they stepped through the doorway, the golden light from the chamber flickered out, leaving them in total darkness. The sounds of their footsteps echoed in the narrow corridor, each step feeling heavier than the last.

But one thing was certain—the trial had only just begun.

CHAPTER 3

LABYRINTH OF TIME

The darkness enveloped them as they stepped through the doorway, the air growing cooler with every step. The corridor was narrow and winding, the stone walls slick with moisture. Their footsteps echoed eerily, as if the corridor were alive and listening. Emma's hand tightened around the compass, its vibrations faint but persistent.

"I really hope this isn't another endless maze," Zoe muttered, her voice bouncing off the walls. "We've had enough of those to last a lifetime."

"Let's stay focused," Emma said, her eyes scanning the passage ahead. "The guardians said the trial would test us. That means there's something we're supposed to figure out here."

The corridor widened suddenly, spilling them into a vast chamber. The air buzzed with static energy, and glowing blue symbols lit up along the walls and floor. The room wasn't empty—at its center stood a massive sundial-like structure, its face etched with concentric circles divided by ancient symbols. Above the sundial, faint golden threads of light formed a shifting constellation that mirrored the map they'd seen earlier.

"This... doesn't look like a maze," Rami said, stepping closer to the sundial. He peered at the symbols. "Looks more like... a puzzle?"

As soon as he spoke, the air in the room changed. A low hum filled the space, and the walls began to shimmer. The symbols glowed brighter, and the golden threads above them shifted rapidly, almost as if they were alive.

Emma stepped closer to the sundial, her heart racing. "It's a test of time," she whispered, running her fingers over the etched circles. "These symbols... they're markers of different moments. We have to align them somehow."

"Align them to what?" Liam asked, glancing nervously at the glowing walls.

"The compass," Emma said, holding it up. Its needle spun wildly for a moment before locking into place. "It's guiding us. We just have to figure out what it's pointing to."

Zoe crouched beside the sundial, studying the symbols. "They're all different. Look—some of these look like star patterns, but others... they look like phases of the moon or suns."

"And here," Rami said, pointing to the outermost circle, "these look like years or ages. Like different points in history."

Emma's mind raced. The sundial wasn't just a puzzle—it was a timeline, a map of moments. "We need to align these symbols to match the sequence of events we've encountered so far," she said.

The room suddenly trembled, and a booming voice echoed around them, the words incomprehensible but filled with urgency. The golden threads above them began to shift, snapping into new constellations that formed briefly before vanishing again.

"Okay, no pressure," Zoe muttered. "Let's just rearrange the history of the universe before this whole place collapses."

Working together, they began moving the sundial's rings. Each ring was heavy, grinding against the others as they shifted the symbols into place. Emma focused on the inner circle, aligning the star patterns with what she remembered from the murals. Rami and Liam worked on the outer circles, deciphering the ages and aligning them to the compass's direction. Zoe stayed on high alert, watching the room for any signs of danger.

As the final ring clicked into place, the hum grew louder, and the golden threads above them snapped into a single, glowing constellation. The air vibrated, and the symbols on the sundial lit up in a cascade of light.

"Did we do it?" Rami asked, stepping back as the sundial began to glow.

Before anyone could answer, the ground beneath their feet shifted. The sundial began to sink into the floor, revealing a hidden staircase spiraling downward.

"Well, that's not ominous at all," Zoe said, peering into the dark void below.

Emma took a deep breath. "It's the only way forward. The compass is still pulling us this way."

They descended the staircase, the walls around them illuminated by faint blue light. As they reached the bottom, they entered another chamber—smaller than the last, but even more intricate.

In the center of the room stood a pedestal holding a small, glowing orb. The orb pulsated with a golden light, and around it, more symbols swirled in the air like fireflies.

"This must be part of the trial," Emma said, stepping closer. The moment her hand touched the pedestal, the room sprang to life. The swirling symbols began to form shapes—images of the past and future.

They saw flashes of the lost city in its prime: bustling streets, towering structures, and people moving with purpose. But then the images changed, showing destruction—buildings collapsing, the people vanishing, and the city falling into ruin.

"It's like a warning," Liam said, his voice hushed.

Emma nodded. "The city wasn't just lost to time. It was destroyed by something... or someone."

The orb glowed brighter, and the symbols reformed into a single image: the spiral they had seen before. Emma felt a jolt of recognition. "The spiral... it's more than just a symbol. It's connected to everything—the compass, the stones, and the city itself."

Before they could react, the orb flashed, and the pedestal began to sink into the floor. The walls trembled, and the sound of grinding stone filled the air.

"Uh, I think that's our cue to leave!" Rami shouted.

They ran back toward the staircase, the chamber collapsing behind them. As they climbed, the golden orb reappeared in Emma's hand, glowing faintly.

When they finally emerged back into the main hall, the guardians were waiting. The leader stepped forward, his masked face unreadable.

"You have passed the first trial," he said, his voice resonating with power. "But the path ahead will be even more treacherous."

Emma glanced at her friends, their faces a mix of exhaustion and determination. They had survived the labyrinth, but she knew the hardest part was yet to come.

CHAPTER 4

WHISPERS OF THE ANCIENTS

The guardians moved in silent unison, their staffs glowing as they gestured for the group to follow. The massive hall behind them now felt like a distant memory, the air ahead carrying an even heavier tension. Emma clutched the golden orb, its faint warmth a reminder of what they had just overcome.

"First trial?" Rami muttered, glancing at the leader. "How many are there?"

The leader's voice was calm but cryptic. "As many as the city deems necessary. Time reveals all."

"Comforting," Zoe said under her breath, adjusting her satchel. "Let's just hope we don't have to fight any ancient monsters."

The group followed the guardians through a new corridor that opened into a chamber unlike anything they had seen before. The walls were alive with movement—shadows of people bustling through a city, shimmering like ghostly projections. Laughter, music, and the clatter of daily life echoed faintly, as if they had stepped back into the city's golden age.

"What is this?" Liam asked, staring at the vibrant scenes. "Are these... memories?"

Emma approached the nearest wall, where an image of a craftsman carving a large stone was unfolding. His hands moved with precision, but his face was tense, as though he knew something was coming.

"It's like we're seeing their lives," she said, her voice tinged with awe. "Before everything fell apart."

The guardians halted abruptly at the chamber's center. One of them turned, his voice sharp. "Do not lose yourselves in the past. Focus on the path."

Easier said than done. The shadows shifted again, this time showing a council of robed figures standing around a massive table. They argued passionately, pointing to a glowing map of the city. The edges of the map flickered with cracks of light, like the beginning of an earthquake.

"Something tore this place apart," Emma said softly, her eyes fixed on the figures.

"It wasn't just time," Rami added. "It was something bigger—maybe even magical."

The orb in Emma's hand pulsed, and the voices of the council became clearer, their words forming fragments of warnings:

"The stones must remain hidden..."
"If the spiral collapses, all is lost..."
"We must prepare for the end..."

Before the group could make sense of it, the glowing walls dimmed, and the room fell silent. One of the guardians stepped forward, lifting his staff. The floor beneath them rumbled, and a large section began to slide away, revealing a staircase spiraling downward into darkness.

"Another staircase," Zoe said, her tone dripping with sarcasm. "What a surprise."

But this one felt different. The air emanating from below was colder, heavier, and carried a strange hum that resonated in their chests.

"Stay close," Emma said as they descended.

At the bottom of the stairs, they found themselves in a cavernous room with no visible ceiling. The floor was smooth and reflective, like a pool of black glass, and above them floated glowing orbs, each containing what appeared to be fragments of the past.

"This is... incredible," Liam whispered, staring at the floating orbs.

One orb showed a family laughing together as they shared a meal. Another showed a craftsman chiseling a tablet. But some were darker—buildings crumbling, people fleeing, and storms ripping through the city.

The guardians didn't move this time. They simply pointed to the largest orb at the room's center, its glow pulsing faintly. Emma stepped closer, her reflection distorted on the black floor.

As she reached out to touch the orb, a sharp voice rang out behind her.

"Careful!" Zoe hissed.

But it was too late. The moment Emma's fingers grazed the orb's surface, it expanded, enveloping the entire group in light.

Inside the Vision

They found themselves standing in the middle of the lost city, but it was alive. The streets buzzed with life. Merchants shouted their wares from colorful market stalls, children dashed between towering stone structures, and the air was filled with a melody played by unseen musicians. The city gleamed under a radiant sun, its golden spires reflecting light like beacons.

"We're... inside the past," Emma whispered, turning in awe.

Zoe reached out to touch a nearby wall, but her hand passed through it as if it were smoke. "We're not really here. This is some kind of projection."

Rami pointed ahead. "Look! Isn't that the council we saw earlier?"

At the center of the square stood the same robed figures they had seen in the shadows. They were gathered around an intricately carved stone altar, each holding a different object—a scroll, a staff, and what looked like a fragment of the spiral symbol.

Emma felt a tug from the golden orb, which now glowed brighter in her hand. "They're the key," she said. "Whatever happened to the city, it started here."

The council's voices became audible, their argument growing more intense.

"The spiral's balance is failing," one of them said. *"The stones cannot hold it together much longer,"* another replied. *"Then we must act now,"* the third insisted. "Hide the stones, scatter them across time if we must."

Before they could hear more, the vision shifted violently. The sky darkened, and the city trembled. People screamed as cracks spread through the streets, and golden spires crumbled into the ground. A swirling vortex of energy erupted in the distance, consuming everything in its path.

"Look at the altar!" Liam shouted.

The altar in the vision began to fracture, the spiral symbol glowing with an eerie red light. The council members frantically performed a ritual, their words drowned out by the chaos around them. One by one, their objects vanished in flashes of light, scattering like shooting stars.

"This is it," Emma said. "This is when they hid the stones."

Suddenly, the vortex surged toward them, and the vision collapsed. The group was flung back into the chamber, gasping for air. The glowing orbs above them flickered before fading completely, plunging the room into darkness.

Aftermath

"What just happened?" Rami panted, clutching his knees.

"We saw the end of the city," Emma said, her voice shaking. "And the beginning of its secrets."

The guardians stepped forward, their glowing staffs lighting the room. "You have seen what was lost," the leader said. "Now, you must decide if you are worthy to find what remains."

Emma held up the golden orb, which now pulsed with a steady light. "We'll find the stones," she said firmly. "And we'll figure out how to stop whatever caused this destruction."

The leader inclined his head. "Then you must face the next trial. The path forward lies within the heart of the spiral."

The floor beneath them shifted once again, and a new doorway opened, revealing another staircase. This one glowed faintly, the spiral symbol etched into each step.

Emma looked at her friends, their faces reflecting a mix of fear and determination. "Ready for whatever's next?"

Zoe smirked. "Do we have a choice?"

As they stepped onto the glowing staircase, the air seemed to hum with anticipation. The next chapter of their journey awaited, and the stakes had never been higher.

CHAPTER 5

THE HEART OF THE SPIRAL

The glowing staircase seemed endless, spiralling down into a cavernous void. Each step illuminated with a faint golden light as the group descended, their breaths echoing in the hollow space. The air grew cooler and heavier, carrying an almost tangible energy that prickled their skin.

"This is different," Liam said, running his fingers along the smooth walls etched with intricate patterns. "It feels... alive."

"Not exactly comforting," Zoe muttered, glancing nervously at the shifting designs.

Emma led the way, her grip tight on the golden orb. Its glow intensified with each step, casting long shadows around them. The compass strapped to her belt vibrated faintly, its needle spinning erratically.

"What's wrong with it?" Rami asked, noticing the erratic movements.

"It's reacting to something," Emma replied. "Something powerful."

After what felt like hours, the staircase opened into a massive underground chamber. The ceiling stretched impossibly high, shimmering with veins of gold and silver light. At the centre of the room was a colossal spiral carved into the floor, its grooves filled with a glowing, liquid-like substance that pulsed like a heartbeat.

"This must be the heart of the spiral," Emma said, her voice barely above a whisper.

The room thrummed with energy, the vibrations rattling their bones. Around the spiral were towering pillars, each adorned with carvings that depicted moments from the city's history. Some showed its creation, others its rise to power, and finally, its catastrophic fall.

"What are we supposed to do here?" Zoe asked, stepping cautiously toward the spiral.

As if in response, the golden orb in Emma's hand flared brightly. The liquid within the spiral began to swirl, and a voice—ancient and deep—reverberated through the chamber.

"Seek the truth within the spiral. Only then will the path reveal itself."

The liquid formed images, shifting like a living tapestry. The group saw flashes of the city's history, but this time, the images lingered on specific events.

In one scene, the council members stood together, holding the spiral stones. Their faces were grim as they passed the stones to hooded figures, who vanished into portals of light.

In another, a shadowy figure loomed over the city, its form indistinct but menacing. Its outstretched hands sent tendrils of darkness curling through the streets, consuming everything in their path.

"Who is that?" Rami asked, his voice shaking.

"No idea," Emma said. "But I think they're why the stones were scattered."

The final image showed the spiral itself cracking, the glowing liquid spilling out and spreading like veins through the city. The light dimmed, and the chamber fell silent once more.

The Test of Courage

Before they could process what they'd seen, the ground beneath them trembled. The pillars around the room began to move, twisting and reshaping themselves into humanoid figures. They were massive, their stone bodies crackling with energy. Their eyes glowed with the same golden light as the spiral.

"Tell me those aren't what I think they are," Zoe groaned, backing up.

"They're guardians," Emma said, her voice steady despite her racing heart. "Another trial."

The largest of the stone figures stepped forward, its deep voice resonating through the chamber. "The spiral tests all who seek its secrets. Prove your courage, or be lost to the void."

Without warning, the figures charged.

"Scatter!" Emma shouted.

The group split up, dodging the lumbering stone guardians. Emma darted toward the spiral, clutching the orb as if it were a lifeline. The compass buzzed urgently at her side, its needle pointing directly toward the center of the spiral.

"Emma!" Liam called, ducking beneath a guardian's swing. "What are you doing?"

"I think the spiral is the key!" she shouted back. "We have to reach it!"

Rami and Zoe exchanged a look. "Cover her!" Rami said, grabbing a piece of broken stone and hurling it at one of the guardians. It barely flinched, but it turned toward him, giving Emma an opening.

Zoe sprinted to another guardian, using her agility to stay just out of its reach. "Over here, you oversized statue!" she yelled, waving her arms.

Emma reached the edge of the spiral, the liquid's glow almost blinding. The orb in her hand began to resonate, its pulses matching the rhythm of the spiral's movements.

"Come on," she whispered, stepping into the center.

The moment her foot touched the liquid, the guardians froze. The chamber fell silent, and the spiral's glow intensified. The orb in Emma's hand floated into the air, merging with the spiral in a burst of light.

The Spiral's Warning

The light engulfed the room, and the group found themselves suspended in a void of swirling colors. A voice, softer but no less powerful, spoke directly to them.

"You have proven your courage, but the path ahead is fraught with danger. The stones hold the key to restoring balance, but the shadow seeks them as well. Time is not your ally—move swiftly, or all will be lost."

As the voice faded, the group was gently lowered back into the chamber. The guardians had returned to their pillar forms, and the spiral's glow had dimmed.

Emma picked up the orb, now cool to the touch. "We're not just finding the stones," she said, her voice resolute. "We're racing against something—someone—who wants them for the wrong reasons."

"Then we'd better not waste any time," Zoe said, brushing dust off her jacket.

The guardians stepped aside, revealing another staircase leading deeper into the heart of the city. Emma glanced at her friends, their faces tired but determined.

"This is far from over," she said, leading the way down.

CHAPTER 6

THE FORGOTTEN LIBRARY

The staircase led them into a vast underground chamber that took their breath away. Shelves carved from stone towered into the darkness, filled with ancient scrolls, books, and artifacts glowing faintly with an ethereal light. The air was heavy with the scent of aged parchment and magic, as if the room itself was alive with knowledge.

"Is this what I think it is?" Zoe asked, her voice echoing.

"It's a library," Liam whispered. "A massive one."

"A forgotten one," Emma added, her eyes scanning the inscriptions carved into the walls. The symbols were unfamiliar yet strangely comforting, as though they were meant to be understood by anyone who entered.

The guardians hadn't followed them this time. Instead, the group stood alone, their footsteps muffled by the soft, glowing floor as they ventured deeper into the library.

"This place must hold the city's secrets," Rami said, pulling a scroll from the nearest shelf. He unrolled it carefully, revealing detailed diagrams of the spiral symbol and annotations written in a flowing script. "Look at this—it's like a blueprint for the city's magic."

Emma's fingers brushed against a leather-bound book with an embossed spiral on its cover. She opened it to find pages filled with illustrations of the stones they were seeking, each radiating with a unique energy.

"They called them the Anchors of Time," she read aloud. "Each stone was tied to a different era, holding the threads of the city's balance. Without them, the spiral—"

"Collapses," Zoe finished, peering over her shoulder. "That explains why they scattered the stones. But it doesn't explain why the city fell apart."

Before Emma could respond, the floor trembled slightly, and a soft hum filled the air. The shelves closest to them began to shift, rearranging themselves into new configurations.

"What's happening?" Liam asked, backing away from the moving shelves.

"I think it's reacting to us," Emma said. She clutched the golden orb, which pulsed faintly in her hand. "It's trying to guide us."

The Guide Appears

As the shelves settled, a glowing figure emerged from the center of the library. It was humanoid but translucent, its form flickering like a flame. Its face was indistinct, but its voice was clear and melodic.

"Seekers of the stones," it said, its tone both welcoming and grave. "You stand within the archives of time, where the memories of the city are preserved. What is it you wish to learn?"

Emma stepped forward, her grip tightening on the orb. "We want to know why the city fell—and how we can find the stones to fix it."

The figure regarded her for a moment before extending its hand. "The truth lies within the core, but the path is perilous. The knowledge you seek comes with a price."

"What kind of price?" Zoe asked warily.

"To uncover the truth, you must face the memories of those who sought to protect the city—and those who sought to destroy it."

The group exchanged uneasy glances. "We don't have a choice," Emma said finally. "We need to know what happened."

The figure nodded, and the room transformed around them. The shelves faded away, replaced by a grand hall filled with people—scholars, warriors, and council members all bustling with purpose.

The Memory Unfolds

The group watched as a young scribe approached the council with a scroll in hand. "The spiral is weakening," he said urgently. "The stones are faltering. We must act now."

One of the council members shook his head. "We cannot disrupt the balance further. The stones must remain as they are."

Another council member slammed his fist on the table. "And if the spiral collapses entirely? We will lose everything!"

The argument escalated until a hooded figure entered the hall, his presence silencing the room. His face was hidden, but his voice carried an unsettling authority.

"There is another way," the figure said, placing a black stone on the table. Its surface shimmered with dark energy, sending a chill through the group.

"That's not one of the spiral stones," Rami muttered.

"No," Emma said, her voice trembling. "It's something else. Something wrong."

The memory shifted again, showing the hooded figure performing a ritual with the black stone. The spiral symbol cracked under the strain, its glow dimming as the city began to tremble.

"He sabotaged it," Liam said, his fists clenched. "He's the reason the city fell apart."

The memory faded, and the group was once again in the library. The glowing figure reappeared, its light dimmer than before.

"The black stone was not of this world," it said. "It corrupted the spiral, forcing the council to scatter the Anchors of Time in a desperate attempt to preserve what little balance remained."

A New Threat

"Wait," Zoe said, her brow furrowed. "If the black stone caused this, what happened to it?"

The figure's light flickered. "The stone was lost with the city. But its power lingers, and there are those who seek to wield it."

Emma's heart sank. "The shadow we saw in the vision. It's looking for the stones—and the black stone."

"Correct," the figure said. "If the shadow gains all the stones, it will restore the spiral—but in its corrupted form, bending time to its will."

"We have to stop it," Emma said firmly. "We'll find the stones first."

The figure nodded. "Then your path lies deeper within the city. But beware—the shadow's presence grows stronger the closer you come to the stones."

The shelves began to shift again, revealing a hidden passageway lined with faintly glowing runes. The figure stepped aside, motioning for them to proceed.

"You carry the burden of time," it said. "May the spiral guide you."

Emma looked at her friends, their faces resolute despite the weight of what they had learned. "Let's go," she said, stepping into the passageway.

As they disappeared into the darkness, the library's glow dimmed, and the hum of ancient energy faded into silence.

CHAPTER 7

THE LABYRINTH OF ECHOES

The glowing runes on the walls of the hidden passageway provided their only light as the group moved cautiously forward. The air was damp and carried a faint metallic tang, and the sound of their footsteps seemed to echo endlessly, as if the tunnel stretched far beyond the limits of their senses.

"Is it just me, or do these echoes sound... off?" Zoe asked, stopping to listen.

Emma nodded, her face tense. "It's like they're not ours. Almost like something else is mimicking us."

"That's comforting," Rami muttered, gripping a sturdy branch he'd found in the library to use as a makeshift weapon.

The tunnel suddenly opened up into an expansive chamber, its floor a polished, reflective surface that mirrored the room above it. The walls were lined with countless stone doors, each marked with a symbol. Above them, a massive, intricately carved dome sparkled with thousands of tiny lights, like a map of the stars.

"Wow," Liam said, his voice filled with awe. "It's beautiful."

"And confusing," Emma said, scanning the chamber. "Which door are we supposed to take?"

The Voice of the Past

Before anyone could answer, the air grew heavy, and a faint, melodic hum filled the chamber. The reflective floor shimmered, and their own reflections began to move independently, stepping out of the surface and forming solid, spectral versions of themselves.

"Okay, nope," Zoe said, backing away from her doppelgänger, whose expression mirrored hers with unsettling precision.

"Is this a test, or are we just in way over our heads?" Liam asked, watching his spectral twin draw a sword made of glowing light.

The shimmering versions of the group moved in unison, blocking their path to the stone doors. A voice, deep and resonant, filled the chamber.

"Only those who understand their true selves may pass. Face your fears, or be lost in the labyrinth forever."

The spectral figures lunged, forcing the group into action.

A Battle of Reflection

Emma's doppelgänger moved with calculated precision, mirroring her every move with an almost mocking grace. As Emma dodged a glowing blade aimed at her, she realized brute force wouldn't win this battle.

"It's not about fighting them!" she shouted to the others. "We have to figure out what they represent!"

"Easy for you to say," Rami called, narrowly avoiding a strike from his double. "This guy is out for blood!"

"Then stop fighting him and listen!" Emma said, standing still and facing her twin.

Her doppelgänger paused, its glowing eyes locking onto hers. For a moment, the room seemed to fall silent. Emma thought about everything she'd faced so far—the uncertainty, the responsibility, the fear of failing her friends.

"You're not my enemy," she said quietly. "You're my fear. My doubt."

The doppelgänger's weapon dissolved, and it bowed before stepping back into the reflective floor, vanishing without a trace.

"It worked!" Liam shouted, watching Emma's twin disappear.

"Great, so I just have to have a heartfelt chat with my evil twin while it's trying to kill me," Zoe quipped, dodging a swipe.

Emma turned to help the others, calling out, "Think about what's been holding you back! Face it head-on!"

Breaking Through

One by one, the group confronted their fears:

- **Zoe's twin** represented her fear of letting people down, of not being fast or strong enough when it mattered most. She admitted that she didn't always have to be perfect, and her double faded away.

- **Rami's twin** mirrored his fear of being powerless, of not contributing enough to the team. He realized his worth wasn't tied to physical strength but to his quick thinking and resourcefulness.

- **Liam's twin** embodied his fear of losing control, of making a mistake that would cost someone dearly. He accepted that mistakes were part of being human, and his twin vanished.

With the spectral figures gone, the chamber grew still, and the deep voice returned.

"You have faced yourselves and prevailed. The path is open."

Choosing the Door

The symbols on the stone doors began to glow, but only one remained lit—a spiral surrounded by rays of light.

"Guess that's our door," Rami said, pointing to it.

Emma approached the door, hesitating before placing her hand on the glowing symbol. The stone shifted and groaned as it slid open, revealing another staircase leading down.

"Deeper we go," Zoe said, her voice betraying a mix of excitement and apprehension.

As they descended, the reflective floor began to ripple, as though watching them leave.

CHAPTER 8

THE CHAMBER OF WHISPERS

The staircase spiralled down into an unsettling quiet. The deeper they went, the thicker the air seemed to grow, filled with an unspoken weight. A faint, rhythmic sound accompanied them—soft whispers that seemed to emanate from the very walls.

"Does anyone else hear that?" Zoe asked, her voice barely above a whisper.

"I hear it," Liam replied, clutching his flashlight tighter. "But it's not... words. Just noise."

"It's like it's trying to talk to us," Emma said, glancing at the golden orb in her hand. Its glow had dimmed, as if the energy around them was overwhelming it.

At last, the staircase opened into a cavernous hall. Massive pillars carved with spirals and strange symbols rose into the shadows above, and the floor was covered in a mosaic that seemed to shift when viewed from different angles. At the center of the room stood a pedestal, and atop it lay a glowing, red gemstone—the first of the Anchors of Time.

"We found it," Rami said, his voice filled with awe. "The first stone."

"Don't celebrate yet," Emma warned. "This feels too easy."

The Voices Take Shape

As they approached the pedestal, the whispers grew louder, coalescing into distinct voices. Each one spoke in a different tone, but their words were the same:

"Turn back. The price is too great. Leave while you can."

"I don't like this," Zoe said, backing away.

Before anyone could respond, the whispers intensified, and the shadows in the room began to shift. Dark figures emerged, their forms fluid and ever-changing, like living shadows with glowing eyes. They surrounded the group, cutting off any escape.

"What are these things?" Liam asked, pulling Zoe behind him.

"I think they're the whispers," Emma said, her eyes scanning the figures. "They don't want us to take the stone."

The largest shadow stepped forward, its voice deeper and more menacing than the rest.

"The stones do not belong to you. Leave now, or be consumed."

A Battle of Conviction

The group braced themselves as the shadows surged forward.

"Defensive formation!" Rami shouted, grabbing a piece of rubble to use as a weapon.

Emma held the orb tightly, its faint glow providing some comfort. "We can't fight them like this. They're not solid!"

"Then how do we stop them?" Zoe asked, dodging a shadowy tendril that lashed out at her.

Emma thought back to the library and the trials they'd faced so far. "They're testing us again. It's not about strength—it's about proving we're worthy of the stone!"

"How do we do that?" Liam shouted, struggling to hold his ground against a swarm of smaller shadows.

"Hold your ground!" Emma called. "Show them we're not afraid!"

The group formed a tight circle, standing firm as the shadows closed in. Emma raised the golden orb high above her head, focusing all her energy on its faint glow.

"We're here to restore the spiral," she said loudly, her voice steady. "We're not leaving without the stone."

The largest shadow loomed over her, its glowing eyes narrowing.

"Prove it."

The Test of Sacrifice

The shadows withdrew slightly, forming a ring around the pedestal. The largest figure gestured toward the glowing stone.

50

"To claim the stone, one must prove their commitment. What will you sacrifice for the balance of time?"

Emma hesitated, her heart pounding. What could she offer that would satisfy the shadows? She looked at her friends, their faces filled with determination despite the fear in their eyes.

Finally, she stepped forward, holding the orb out toward the pedestal. "Take this," she said. "It's guided us this far, but if giving it up means saving the spiral, then so be it."

The shadow paused, its gaze fixed on the orb. The room grew silent as the other shadows seemed to lean in, waiting.

After a long moment, the largest shadow spoke.

"Your sacrifice is accepted. The stone is yours. But be warned—this is only the beginning."

Claiming the Stone

The shadows dissolved into the air, leaving the room eerily quiet. The group approached the pedestal cautiously, and Emma picked up the glowing red stone.

The moment her fingers touched it, a surge of energy coursed through her, and the room seemed to pulse with light.

The mosaic on the floor began to shift, revealing a map of the city with glowing pathways leading to other locations. One path in particular glowed brighter than the others, leading to the next stone.

"Looks like we know where to go next," Rami said, examining the map.

Emma nodded, slipping the red stone into her bag. "But we need to be careful. Whatever's guarding the next stone won't make it easy for us."

As they prepared to leave the chamber, the whispers returned, softer this time.

"The shadow grows stronger. Beware the black stone."

Emma shivered, glancing back at the now-empty pedestal. "Let's keep moving. We've got a long way to go."

With the first stone in their possession and the map guiding their way, the group stepped back into the labyrinth, their resolve stronger than ever.

CHAPTER 9

THE FORGOTTEN CITY

The map's glowing path led them out of the labyrinth and back into the city's ancient streets. But something had changed. The city was no longer quiet; it buzzed with a strange, unsettling energy. The air shimmered, and the buildings seemed to warp and twist as if caught in a dream.

"This place feels... alive," Zoe said, her eyes scanning the shifting skyline.

"It's like the city's watching us," Rami added, gripping his flashlight tightly.

Emma studied the map. The glowing path led toward the heart of the city, where a towering ziggurat rose into the sky. Unlike the other ruins, the ziggurat was pristine, its surface gleaming with intricate carvings that seemed to move under the sunlight.

"That's where the map is leading us," Emma said, pointing toward the structure.

Liam frowned. "It looks like it's in perfect condition. Why hasn't it aged like everything else?"

"I don't think it's part of this world," Emma replied, her voice low. "It's connected to the stones—and to the spiral."

The Streets Come Alive

As they moved closer to the ziggurat, the city's energy became more erratic. The ground trembled, and the warped buildings seemed to lean toward them, their crumbling facades taking on vaguely humanoid shapes.

"I don't like this," Zoe said, keeping close to the group.

"Neither do I," Emma admitted. "Stay together. We're almost there."

Suddenly, the ground in front of them cracked open, and a massive, glowing fissure appeared. From it rose a creature unlike anything they ever seen—a towering, shifting mass of stone and light, its form constantly changing.

"What is that?" Rami shouted, stumbling backward.

"It's a guardian," Emma said, recognizing the creature from the ancient texts she'd seen in the library. "It's here to stop us."

The creature roared, its voice a deep, resonant hum that shook the ground. It raised a massive, glowing arm and slammed it down, narrowly missing the group.

"Run!" Liam shouted, pulling Zoe with him as the group scattered.

Outsmarting the Guardian

The creature pursued them relentlessly, its massive form tearing through the city as if it were weightless. The group ducked and weaved through the streets, but it quickly became clear they couldn't outrun it.

"We have to stop it!" Emma shouted.

"And how do we do that?" Rami called back. "It's made of rock!"

Emma glanced at the glowing red stone in her bag. An idea sparked. "The stones are connected to the spiral! Maybe we can use this against it!"

Dodging another strike from the creature, Emma pulled the red stone from her bag. Its glow intensified, pulsing in time with the creature's movements.

"It's reacting to the stone!" Liam said, noticing the change.

Emma turned to the others. "We need to lure it into the fissure. If the stones are connected, it might be drawn to the energy there!"

Zoe nodded. "I'll distract it. You get ready to use the stone."

A Daring Plan

While Zoe led the creature away, Emma, Rami, and Liam positioned themselves near the glowing fissure. The ground trembled as the creature closed in, its massive form casting a long shadow over them.

Emma held the stone aloft, its glow so bright now that it illuminated the entire street. The creature stopped, its shifting form trembling as it focused on the stone.

"It's working," Emma whispered.

"Now what?" Rami asked.

"Now we make it fall," Emma said, stepping closer to the edge of the fissure. "Hey! Over here!"

The creature roared and lunged toward her, its massive arms outstretched. At the last second, Emma threw the stone into the fissure and dove out of the way.

The creature hesitated, its form trembling as if caught between two forces. Then, with a deafening roar, it plunged into the fissure, its glowing form disappearing into the depths.

The city grew still.

A Message in the Ruins

The fissure closed, and the red stone floated back up, now glowing even brighter. Emma caught it, relief washing over her.

"That was way too close," Rami said, helping her to her feet.

"Agreed," Zoe added, joining them.

As the group approached the ziggurat, they noticed new carvings appearing on its surface. The symbols formed a sequence of images: the glowing red stone, the ziggurat, and a second stone—this one blue—resting in a different location.

"It's a clue," Emma said, studying the carvings. "The second stone must be there."

Liam pointed to a symbol at the bottom of the carving: a swirling black void surrounded by jagged lines. "And that's... not good."

Emma's stomach sank. The symbol reminded her of the warning from the labyrinth.

"Beware the black stone."

"Whatever's next," she said, slipping the red stone back into her bag, "we need to be ready."

With the first stone secured and a new destination revealed, the group climbed the steps of the ziggurat, their resolve stronger than ever.

CHAPTER 10

THE SKYBOUND PASSAGE

The steps of the ziggurat seemed to stretch endlessly upward. As the group ascended, they noticed the air changing—it grew thinner, charged with a strange energy that made their skin tingle. The carvings on the walls began to glow faintly, their intricate designs pulsating in rhythm with the red stone in Emma's bag.

"How high is this thing?" Zoe asked, pausing to catch her breath.

Rami peered over the edge, his face turning pale. "Too high. Let's not look down."

"Keep moving," Emma urged. "We're almost at the top."

The group finally reached the summit, where a flat platform awaited them. At the center was an archway made of smooth, reflective stone, its surface rippling like water. Symbols matching the ones on the first stone were etched along its frame, glowing faintly.

"Is this a portal?" Liam asked, stepping closer.

Emma nodded. "It must be. It's how we'll reach the next location."

"But how do we activate it?" Rami asked, glancing around.

Emma pulled out the red stone. As soon as it left her bag, the archway responded, its surface shimmering brighter.

"Looks like the stone is the key," she said.

Through the Portal

Emma held the stone near the archway, and the rippling surface solidified into a bright, swirling vortex. A faint hum filled the air, growing louder as the portal stabilized.

"Are we really doing this?" Zoe asked, staring at the vortex.

"Do we have a choice?" Liam replied.

Emma stepped forward, taking a deep breath. "Stay close and don't let go of each other. Ready?"

One by one, they stepped into the portal. The sensation was unlike anything they'd ever experienced—weightlessness mixed with a rush of wind and light. Shapes and colors blurred past them, and faint echoes of voices filled their ears.

Then, just as suddenly as it began, the ride ended.

Arrival in the Floating Isles

The group stumbled out of the portal and onto solid ground. But what greeted them was beyond anything they could have imagined.

They stood on a lush, floating island suspended in a vast, endless sky. Other islands hovered nearby, connected by glowing bridges of light. Strange, crystalline trees grew from the ground, their branches shimmering with hues of blue and silver.

"This is incredible," Rami said, spinning around to take it all in.

"Where are we?" Zoe asked, staring at a massive structure in the distance. It resembled a fortress made entirely of glass, perched on the largest of the floating isles.

"That's where we need to go," Emma said, consulting the red stone. Its glow now pulsed in the direction of the fortress.

Danger in the Skies

As they made their way toward the nearest bridge, a sudden screech echoed through the air. Looking up, they saw massive winged creatures circling above—part bird, part reptile, with sharp talons and glowing eyes.

"What are those?" Liam asked, backing away.

"Trouble," Emma said, gripping the stone tightly.

The creatures dove toward them, their screeches piercing the air. The group scattered, narrowly avoiding the sharp talons of the lead beast.

"We can't fight these things!" Rami shouted, dodging another dive.

"Head for the bridge!" Emma called. "We'll be safer on the next island!"

They sprinted toward the glowing bridge, the creatures in hot pursuit. As they stepped onto the bridge, it lit up beneath their feet, emitting a high-pitched hum that seemed to repel the attackers.

"They're not following us!" Zoe said, relief washing over her.

"Let's not question it," Liam replied. "Just keep moving."

A Puzzle to Solve

The group crossed several islands, each more surreal than the last. On one, they encountered a field of floating crystals that chimed softly when touched. On another, they had to navigate a maze of shifting platforms that rearranged themselves with every step.

Finally, they reached the island with the glass fortress. Its towering spires sparkled in the light, and its entrance was guarded by a massive, sealed door covered in symbols.

Emma approached the door, holding up the red stone. As expected, the symbols reacted, glowing faintly. But the door remained closed.

"There must be more to it," she said, examining the carvings.

Zoe pointed to a nearby pedestal. "What's that?"

The pedestal held a small, intricate puzzle made of interlocking pieces that formed a sphere. Beside it was an inscription:

"Only those who understand the balance may proceed."

"It's a test," Emma said. "We have to solve it to get inside."

Balancing the Sphere

The group worked together, carefully manipulating the puzzle pieces. Each movement caused the sphere to emit a soft hum, and the glowing symbols on the door shifted in response.

"It's like the labyrinth," Rami said. "We have to get the pieces into the right alignment."

"But what's the right alignment?" Liam asked, studying the sphere.

Emma thought back to the map and the carvings they'd seen earlier. "The spiral," she said. "It's always about the spiral."

Following her intuition, they arranged the pieces into a spiral pattern. As the final piece clicked into place, the sphere glowed brightly, and the massive door slowly opened.

The group exchanged nervous glances before stepping inside.

Inside the Glass Fortress

The interior of the fortress was even more breathtaking than the outside. Walls of shimmering glass reflected endless fractals of light, and a faint melody filled the air. At the center of the chamber floated the second stone—a brilliant blue gem that seemed to pulse with its own rhythm.

"We found it," Emma said, stepping forward.

But before she could reach the stone, the melody shifted, and the walls began to ripple. A figure emerged from the glass—a guardian unlike any they had faced before. Its form was humanoid but translucent, and its eyes glowed with an intense blue light.

"You must prove your worth," the guardian said, its voice echoing through the chamber.

The group braced themselves for the next challenge, knowing that the hardest part of their journey was still ahead.

CHAPTER 11

THE GUARDIAN'S CHALLENGE

The translucent guardian stepped forward, its form glimmering like a living shard of glass. Its movements were fluid, almost hypnotic, and its glowing eyes fixed on Emma and her friends.

"You have entered the realm of balance," it intoned. "To claim the second stone, you must demonstrate harmony of mind, body, and spirit."

"Great, another cryptic challenge," Rami muttered.

The guardian raised an arm, and the chamber around them began to transform. The walls of glass shimmered and shifted, creating three distinct paths, each glowing with a different color—gold, silver, and bronze.

"Each of you must face a trial," the guardian said. "Succeed, and the stone will be yours. Fail, and you will remain here, bound to the spiral forever."

"Bound? Like prisoners?" Zoe asked, her voice trembling.

"Or worse," Liam muttered, stepping closer to Emma.

Emma squared her shoulders. "We don't have a choice. Let's do this."

The Trial of the Mind

Emma stepped onto the gold path, and the world around her shifted into a vast, endless library. The shelves stretched to infinity, filled with ancient, glowing tomes. At the center of the space stood a pedestal, upon which rested a single, black book.

A disembodied voice filled the air: "To pass this trial, you must decipher the riddle of the spiral."

The black book opened, and glowing symbols began to float out of its pages, forming a complex pattern in the air. Emma recognized the spiral motif but noticed gaps in the sequence. She had to rearrange the symbols to complete it.

Sweat beaded on her brow as she worked, moving symbols around with her hands. Each incorrect move caused the pattern to destabilize, sending shards of light flying through the air.

"Focus, Emma," she whispered to herself, recalling the lessons from the labyrinth. The spiral was not just a shape—it was a balance of forces.

With a final adjustment, the pattern clicked into place. The spiral glowed brightly, and the library dissolved, returning her to the chamber.

"You have proven your mind," the guardian said, bowing slightly.

The Trial of the Body

Liam's silver path led him to a narrow bridge suspended over a seemingly bottomless chasm. Strong winds whipped around him, threatening to knock him off balance.

"Great. Heights and wind. My favorite," he grumbled.

The disembodied voice returned. "To pass this trial, you must cross without falling. But beware—the bridge will test your strength."

Liam took a cautious step forward, and the bridge began to sway violently. Large chunks of it started falling away, leaving him with only narrow beams to traverse.

As he balanced on the beams, the winds grew stronger, and glowing orbs of energy began flying toward him.

"Seriously?!" he shouted, ducking and weaving to avoid the orbs.

He drew on his agility and determination, leaping from beam to beam, dodging the attacks. With one final jump, he reached the other side, landing hard but safe.

The silver path dissolved, and Liam found himself back in the chamber.

"You have proven your body," the guardian said.

The Trial of the Spirit

Zoe stepped onto the bronze path and found herself standing in a field of mirrors. Each one reflected a version of herself, but the images were distorted— some showing her fears, others her dreams.

"To pass this trial, you must face your true self," the voice said.

Zoe took a deep breath and approached the first mirror. It showed her failing to help her friends, trapped in a spiral of helplessness.

"I'm stronger than that," she said, stepping through the mirror.

The second mirror showed her standing alone, her friends gone. Tears welled up in her eyes, but she clenched her fists.

"I won't let fear control me."

As she moved through the final mirror, it showed her standing with her friends, holding the second stone. She reached out, and the image became reality. The mirrors shattered, and she returned to the chamber.

"You have proven your spirit," the guardian said.

The Stone of Balance

With all three trials complete, the paths disappeared, and the group stood together again in the center of the chamber. The guardian stepped aside, revealing the glowing blue stone.

"You have demonstrated the harmony required to wield the second stone," it said. "But beware—your journey grows more perilous with each step. The spiral will not forgive failure."

Emma stepped forward and carefully picked up the blue stone. Its glow intensified, and she felt a surge of energy coursing through her.

"We did it," she said, turning to the others.

"Barely," Liam muttered, rubbing his sore shoulder.

As they prepared to leave, the guardian spoke again: "The path forward lies in the shadow of the black stone. Only with unity can you hope to prevail."

The group exchanged uneasy glances.

"Sounds like our next destination," Emma said, slipping the blue stone into her bag beside the red one.

With the second stone secured, the group stepped back through the portal, ready to face whatever lay ahead.

CHAPTER 12

SHADOWS OF THE BLACK STONE

The swirling vortex of the portal deposited Emma and her friends back on solid ground, but something was different this time. They found themselves in a dark, misty forest. The air was heavy, and the faint sounds of distant whispers filled the space.

"Where are we now?" Rami asked, shivering as the mist seemed to cling to his skin.

Emma pulled out the blue stone, which glowed faintly in the dense fog. "I don't know, but it doesn't feel welcoming."

"Understatement of the year," Liam muttered, glancing nervously at the shifting shadows among the trees.

As they started walking, the forest seemed to close in around them, the whispers growing louder. Shapes flickered at the edge of their vision—dark figures that vanished when they turned to look directly at them.

"We need to find a way out," Zoe said, gripping her backpack straps tightly.

The Path Revealed

Emma stopped suddenly, her eyes fixed on a faint glow ahead. "Look—there's something up there."

Cautiously, the group moved toward the light, which resolved into a stone altar surrounded by runes carved into the forest floor. On the altar sat a small, black orb, its surface swirling with an inky darkness that seemed to absorb the light around it.

"Is that the black stone?" Rami asked, stepping closer.

Emma shook her head. "It's not glowing like the other stones. But it might be a clue."

The moment Emma reached for the orb, the runes flared to life, and the shadows around them solidified into humanoid forms with glowing red eyes.

"Not again," Liam groaned, pulling the group into a defensive circle.

A Battle of Shadows

The shadow figures advanced, their movements swift and erratic. Emma held up the blue stone, its glow intensifying and pushing back the shadows momentarily.

"They're afraid of the light!" she shouted.

The group worked together, using their environment to their advantage. Liam grabbed a branch and used it to scatter the figures, while Zoe found a shard of crystal from the altar, which reflected the blue stone's light and amplified it.

"Keep them back!" Rami yelled, as he and Emma tried to decipher the runes on the altar.

"Balance," Emma muttered, remembering the guardian's words. She placed both the blue and red stones on the altar, aligning them with the central black orb.

The moment they connected, the stones flared brightly, and the shadow figures froze in place before dissolving into mist.

A Glimpse of the Future

With the shadows gone, the black orb began to change, its surface turning clear to reveal a map inside. Lines of light connected several points, tracing paths across a massive spiral pattern. At the center of the spiral was a glowing black stone.

"That's where we're going next," Emma said, tracing the lines with her finger.

"But look," Zoe said, pointing to one of the glowing points on the map. It showed a scene of a sprawling desert city under siege, with towering black obelisks rising from the sands.

"What is that?" Rami asked, his voice uneasy.

"A warning," Emma said, her voice heavy. "Something's coming, and it's tied to the black stone."

The orb dissolved, leaving behind a small shard of black crystal. Emma pocketed it carefully, knowing it would be important for their next journey.

A Dark Horizon

As they left the altar, the mist began to clear, revealing a new portal shimmering in the distance.

"This is it," Emma said. "The path to the black stone."

"Do we even want to go there?" Liam asked, eyeing the portal warily.

"We don't have a choice," Emma said. "If we don't find it, someone else will. And if the wrong people get their hands on these stones…" She didn't finish her sentence, but the weight of her words hung in the air.

The group stood together, gazing at the portal. They knew that the next step in their journey would be the most dangerous yet.

With a deep breath, Emma led the way, stepping into the portal and vanishing into the swirling light. One by one, her friends followed.

As the portal closed behind them, the faint sound of whispers returned, echoing through the empty forest.

Milton Keynes UK
Ingram Content Group UK Ltd.
UKHW030858011224
451693UK00001B/281